GROSSET & DUNLAP
An imprint of Penguin Random House LLC
1745 Broadway, New York, New York, 10019

First published in the United States of America by Grosset & Dunlap, an imprint of Penguin Random House LLC, 2024

Copyright © 2024 by Penguin Random House LLC

Based on the book THE LITTLE ENGINE THAT COULD (The Complete, Original Edition) by Watty Piper, illustrated by George & Doris Hauman, © Penguin Random House LLC. The Little Engine That Could®, I Think I Can®, and all related titles, logos, and characters are trademarks of Penguin Random House LLC. All rights reserved.

Penguin supports copyright. Copyright fuels creativity, encourages diverse voices, promotes free speech, and creates a vibrant culture. Thank you for buying an authorized edition of this book and for complying with copyright laws by not reproducing, scanning, or distributing any part of it in any form without permission. You are supporting writers and allowing Penguin to continue to publish books for every reader.

GROSSET & DUNLAP is a registered trademark of Penguin Random House LLC.

Visit us online at penguinrandomhouse.com.

Library of Congress Cataloging-in-Publication Data is available.

Manufactured in China

ISBN 9780593752999   10 9 8 7 6 5 4 3 2 1 HH

Design by Mary Claire Cruz

THE LITTLE ENGINE THAT COULD SAVES CHRISTMAS

by Meredith Rusu
illustrated by Jill Howarth

Grosset & Dunlap

It's the night before Christmas, and snow is falling all around Little Engine's bay.

Huff, huff, puff, puff! Little Engine's steam makes tiny clouds in the cold. *Santa Claus is coming tomorrow!* she thinks. *I wonder what he will bring?*

Little Engine tucks into her warm and cozy bay.
She's just drifting off to sleep when . . .

Jingle, jingle, jingle!

What was that sound? Could it be?

"Santa Claus?" whispers Little Engine.

But it's not Santa Claus.
It's one of his elves!

"Santa needs your help!" the elf exclaims. "He's come down with the Frosty Frittens!"

"What are the Frosty Frittens?" asks Little Engine.

"It's like a cold!" she explains. "He's too sick to deliver all the presents."

"I would love to help," says Little Engine. "But how will I get to the North Pole?"

The elf winks. "Leave that to me!"

She sprinkles some magic dust, and with a poof and a whirl, Little Engine lifts off the ground.

"This way to the North Pole!" says the elf.

At the North Pole, Little Engine discovers that Santa does indeed have a bad case of the Frosty Frittens.

"Will you be okay, Santa?" she asks.

"I will be just fine," Santa tells her. "But there's no way I can deliver all the presents by morning. Will you help us save Christmas, Little Engine?"

"Yes, I think I can!"

The elves load stacks of gifts and toys and Christmas-morning surprises into Little Engine's cars. Soon, Little Engine and her friends are ready to fly!

Through the wintry sky, Little Engine puffs over the twinkling towns.

"Do you think we can find the right houses for all of the gifts?" asks the giraffe.

Over the horizon, the night sky grows brighter.

"Do you think we can fly fast enough to deliver the presents by morning?" asks Little Engine.

Just before sunrise, Little Engine
drops off the last gift.

"You did it, Little Engine!" says the elf.
"You delivered all the presents. Now get some rest,
and Merry Christmas!"

. . . she finds one last surprise from Santa Claus.

Thank you for saving Christmas, Little Engine! We didn't just think you could do it. We KNEW you could.
Your friend,
Santa Claus

Back in her bay, Little Engine wakes up with a start.

It's Christmas morning!

Her friends are still fast asleep.
And Santa's elf is gone.

Was it all a dream?
Little Engine wonders.

She isn't sure, until . . .